This book belongs to

_____

_____

_____

The Spice Rack

By Lynne Reid Banks

Illustrated by Omri Stephenson

For Debra and Paloma

When Lucy and Peter got married, all their friends and relations gave them lots of presents. Sets of dishes and cutlery and sheets and towels and glasses and bowls and jugs and pots and pans and...

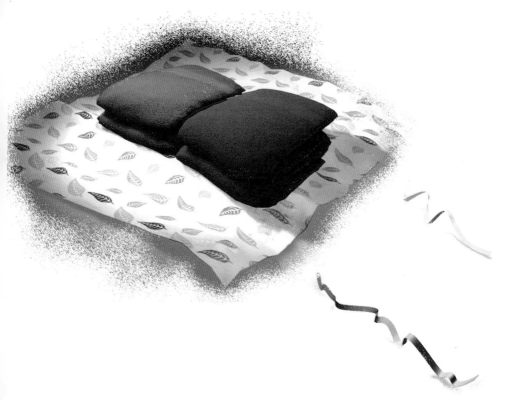

...well, all sorts of lovely things for their new home!

One of the small things they were given was a spice rack. It had six little jars in it. Lucy and Peter weren't very impressed when they opened it, and maybe you wouldn't think it was a very exciting present. But you'd be wrong, and so were Lucy and Peter!

The jars were full of magic. Wonderful dried leaves and powders to give food exciting tastes. No witch or fairy could have thought of a spell to make food taste better than what was in those six little jars.

There was Patika Paprika, Molly Mint and Gerard Garlic in the top row. And underneath them were Charlie Chives, Jamala Ginger and Olive Oregano.

Molly Mint, Charlie Chives and Olive Oregano were dried leaves - herbs. Gerard Garlic, Jamala Ginger and Patika Paprika were the powders - spices.

All they longed to do was to get into the right foods to make them taste more delicious and exciting. The trouble was, Lucy wasn't a very exciting cook. Neither was Peter. All they ever added to their food was salt and pepper - oh, and tomato ketchup.

The spices and their jars stood on the ledge and got dusty.

"If Lucy and Peter don't use us soon, sure and we'll lose all our flavour, so we will!" said Molly Mint sadly.

"I'm dyin' to make them some mint sauce for their Irish Lamb!"

"I could make-a their pizzas taste-a so much more delicious!" said Olive Oregano. "In Italy, no one would-a dream of making pizza without me!"

"Cor! What I couldn't do to cheer up one of their boring old salads!" groaned Charlie Chives.

"Moi aussi!" exclaimed Gerard Garlic in his native French. "Oh, eet ees so verrry sad to seet 'ere when I could be making everry-seeng taste so much better!"

"Except ice-cream," murmured Molly, but Gerard pretended not to hear.

"What a pity they don't like Indian food," cried Jamala Ginger. "But they could at least sprinkle me on their melon. I want to shout at them, Try me! Only try me!"

The only one who didn't speak was Patika Paprika and that was because he could only speak Hungarian. But though he was a spice of few words, he was a spice of *action*. He too felt his lovely red paprika beginning to lose its tang. He sat very quietly, thinking what to do before it was too late.

None of the jars was ever even opened.

The salt and pepper, on the other hand, were used every day. They got emptied and filled over and over again. They teased the herbs and spices *rotten*.

When there was nobody in the kitchen, they hopped around in front of the spice rack. Sally Salt would say saltily, "You fancy-pants spices and herbs think nothing can taste good without you! Well, you're wrong. Nobody wants you"

One day, when Lucy and Peter were out, Sally Salt and Perry Pepper began hopping about, jeering at the poor spice jars more than ever.

"Nobody wants you and nobody will!
None of you ever will get a refill!"

They chanted over and over. Molly, Olive, Charlie,
Jamala, Gerard and Patika felt they could stand
it no longer.

And then an amazing thing happened. Patika
suddenly bounced out of the spice rack!

"Follow me!" Patika shouted (in Hungarian, but even if he'd said it in plain English, the others wouldn't have understood.) They were so gobsmacked, they just stood there goggle-eyed!

They had never even known they could move, until they saw Patika jump.

But then Jamala, and after her Gerard, and finally the other three, jumped out after him.

Sally Salt and Perry Pepper were just flabbergasted.
They jumped aside as the six eager jars hopped
past them.

"Where are you off to? You can't go!
You must stay and go with the flow!"
shouted Perry in his peppery way.

"We're running away!" cried Jamala in her gingery
way. "We must find cooks who appreciate
our magic!"

The herbs and spices bounced onto the stool and then onto the floor. Olive and Charlie rolled over and over, but Patika nudged them upright and then led the way to the door.

"Here! Where are you taking us?" shouted Charlie.
Patika didn't bother trying to answer. He'd noticed
long ago that there was a cat-flap in the door. He
took a big bounce and pushed it open with his
screw-top.

"Follow me!" he shouted again - in Hungarian, of
course. But it didn't matter. They all understood at
last that freedom was near.

The trouble was, not all of them could bounce as high as spicy Patika Paprika. Molly couldn't, and neither could Olive.

But Jamala Ginger was pretty spicy herself. And Gerard helped them. He stood under the cat-flap and Jamala shouted:

"Quick, quick! Hop on his lid!"

One by one, Charlie, Molly and Olive hopped on the garlic jar and out through the cat-flap. Then Gerard bounced after them.

Finally, Jamala did a really gingery flying hop and joined the others outside on the path.

"Where do we go now?" they all asked Patika.

But he was already pogo-ing down the street.

They hopped after him. Before long, Molly Mint said, "I smell peas cooking. This is the place for me!" And she went up a path and lay down on the front doorstep.

The man of the house soon walked up the path. He didn't see Molly lying on the step. He put his foot on her - she rolled - and he went flying through the air!

He scrambled to his feet, picked up the jar, and was just going to hurl her angrily away, when he noticed her label.

"Mmmm - mint!" he said. "I could find a use for this."

Before long, Molly was being tilted over a saucepan full of fresh peas.

Gerard was next. "I seenk someone 'ere ees bake bread!" he muttered, and bounced onto the window-sill. The window was open and he hopped on the table.

He managed to unscrew his lid by jamming his top in a half opened drawer and then doing a spin.

He sprinkled himself over a hot buttered baggette while no one was looking.

The people in the house got a lovely surprise when they ate their garlic-bread!

Charlie Chives, still in the street, got a terrible fright! A dog snatched him up as he was hopping along. "Blimey, I'm done for!" he thought.

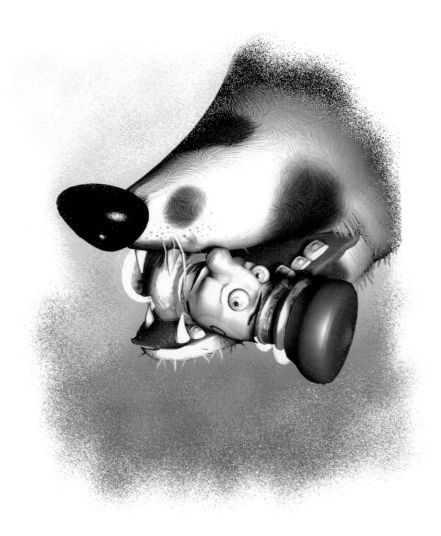

The dog imagined he was some new kind of stick, and carried him home.

The dog owner said, "What have you got there, Bounder? Oh, hey good dog! You've brought me some chives!" He carried Charlie into his kitchen.

"Now hang on, what did I read about chives and tomatoes...?"

And he sprinkled him generously onto a tomato sandwich.

Meanwhile, at the next house, Olive sniffed the air and cried, "Ah! Fresh-a-made pizza! Italians must live-a-here!" and she almost threw herself at the front door.

The young woman who lived there heard her and thought it was a knock. She opened the door. "No one here!" She was about to shut the door when Olive, in desperation, rolled off the step with a clatter.

"Oh, what's this? Someone left oregano here! Just what I need!"

And in a few minutes, Olive was being sprinkled on a pizza just before it was put in the oven.

Mmmm! Oregano magic!

That just left Jamala Ginger and Patika Paprika.
Jamala was puffed. She said, "I do not smell
cooking, but must take a chance. I am a bouncy
spice but still, I cannot hop further!" and she went
into a shop.

A woman was just leaving. She met Jamala in the
doorway and happened to give her a kick. Jamala
rolled under a display basket.

"Oh, my goodness me!" thought Jamala. "I might
stay here for ever, and never get used at all!"

But luckily the woman had spotted her. "Was that a jar of ginger I kicked?" she asked herself, and bending down, she fished Jamala out.

Jamala was carried home in a shopping bag full of interesting food. And before long, she was being shaken into a wonderful cake mixture!

Patika hopped on. He had led the way to freedom, but now even he was tired.

A little boy was riding his bike on the pavement. His front wheel hit Patika, and sent him spinning into the gutter.

He lay there for a long time. Then he felt a sweeper's stiff broom pushing and rolling him along the gutter with a lot of rubbish.

He was lifted on a big shovel and dumped in a bin.
The bin was trundled for a long way.

It was lifted and tipped up. Patika felt himself
falling, falling... He was going to join all the dirt
and litter from the street in a big rubbish-cart.
What a terrible end for a Hungarian spice-hero!

But just as he was falling, a big hand came out and caught him. "What have we here? Why, it is PAPRIKA!" shouted a deep voice. And Patika was held up before a face with a big moustache over a very big smile.

"Finding this is good luck! Tonight I'll have a truly fine Hungarian goulash, just like Mother used to make!"

And would you believe it?
Patika understood every word.
Because the dustman just happened
to be - Hungarian!

ISBN   978-1-4461-3229-6

Designed and published by OGS Designs

www.lynnereidbanks.com
www.ogsdesigns.com